Reading Program Book 3: possessive words

Clifford Does It His Way

by Liz Mills

Illustrated by Gita Lloyd and Eric Binder

Based on the books by Norman Bridwell

SCHOLASTIC INC.
New York Toronto London Auckland Sydney
Mexico City New Delhi Hong Kong Buenos Aires

One day, Emily Elizabeth and her parents walked to the park with Clifford. There was a hot-air balloon at the park and many people wanted to ride in it. Emily Elizabeth and her family already had their tickets to go up in the balloon. Clifford wanted to take the ride, too.

The family stood by the balloon and waited for its owner.

Emily Elizabeth looked in the balloon. How could Clifford ever fit inside? He wanted to take a balloon ride so much. She hoped he could go.

"Hi! This balloon is mine. My name is Ms. Moss," a woman said. "Is this your dog?"

"Yes, he's our dog," Mrs. Howard replied.

Clifford barked, but Ms. Moss shook her head.

"Sorry. He's too big to go," she said.

The balloon rose high into the sky. Clifford looked up. He waved.

"I see your friend Emily Elizabeth," said Cleo. "It takes courage to go up so high."

"Let's chase them!" said Clifford. Clifford, T-Bone, and Cleo chased the balloon across the park. The balloon went higher and higher.

Emily Elizabeth waved to her dog as Ms. Moss began to lower her balloon. Then the balloon stopped. It wouldn't go down and it wouldn't go up. The balloon wouldn't move!

"What happened to my balloon?" asked Ms. Moss. She looked over the side. The balloon was stuck on top of a tree!

"Oh, no!" said Ms. Moss. "I didn't see that branch below my balloon."

Emily Elizabeth saw her Big Red Dog. "Clifford!" she called. "Come help us get out of the tree."

Clifford reached up to the balloon's basket. He pushed the basket out of the tree. But he was still hanging on when it began to float through the air.

When it landed, Emily Elizabeth laughed. "Clifford got a ride on the hot-air balloon after all," she said, "even though...

...Clifford did it his way!"